A Note to Parents and Caregivers:

Read-it! Readers are for children who are just starting on the amazing road to reading. These beautiful books support both the acquisition of reading skills and the love of books.

The PURPLE LEVEL presents basic topics and objects using high frequency words and simple language patterns.

The RED LEVEL presents familiar topics using common words and repeating sentence patterns.

The BLUE LEVEL presents new ideas using a larger vocabulary and varied sentence structure.

The YELLOW LEVEL presents more challenging ideas, a broad vocabulary, and wide variety in sentence structure.

The GREEN LEVEL presents more complex ideas, an extended vocabulary range, and expanded language structures.

The ORANGE LEVEL presents a wide range of ideas and concepts using challenging vocabulary and complex language structures.

When sharing a book with your child, read in short stretches, pausing often to talk about the pictures. Have your child turn the pages and point to the pictures and familiar words. And be sure to reread favorite stories or parts of stories.

There is no right or wrong way to share books with children. Find time to read with your child, and pass on the legacy of literacy.

Adria F. Klein, Ph.D.
Professor Emeritus
California State University
San Bernardino, California

Editor: Jacqueline A. Wolfe
Page Production: Amy Bailey Muehlenhardt
Creative Director: Keith Griffin
Editorial Director: Carol Jones
Managing Editor: Catherine Neitge
The illustrations in this book were created with watercolor and colored pencil.

Picture Window Books
A Capstone Imprint
1710 Roe Crest Drive
North Mankato, MN 56003
www.capstonepub.com

Library of Congress Cataloging-in-Publication Data
Klein, Adria F.
Max goes to the dentist / by Adria F. Klein ; illustrated by Mernie Gallagher-Cole.
p. cm. — (Read-it! readers)
Summary: Max visits the dentist to have his teeth checked and cleaned.
ISBN-13: 978-1-4048-1181-2 (hardcover)
ISBN-10: 1-4048-1181-8 (hardcover)
ISBN-13: 978-1-4048-3061-5 (paperback)
ISBN-10: 1-4048-3061-8 (paperback)
[1. Dentists—Fiction. 2. Hispanic Americans—Fiction.] I. Gallagher-Cole, Mernie, ill. II. Title. III. Series.

PZ7.K678324Mao 2005
[E]—dc22 2005003853

Printed in the United States of America in Eau Claire, Wisconsin.
062014
008315R

Read-it! Readers
Purple Level

Max Goes to the Dentist

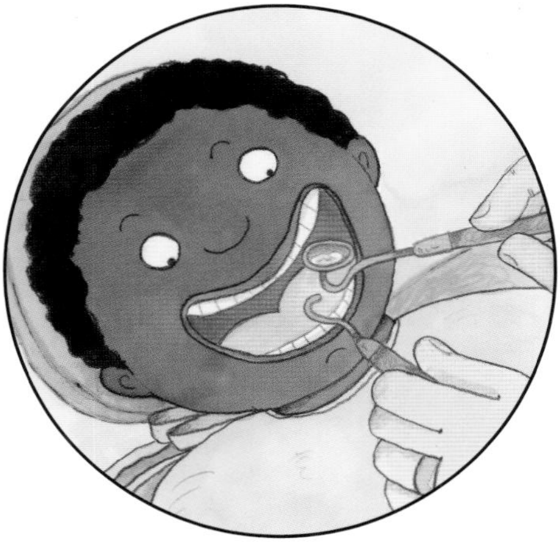

by Adria F. Klein

illustrated by Mernie Gallagher-Cole

Special thanks to our advisers for their expertise:

Adria F. Klein, Ph.D.
Professor Emeritus, California State University
San Bernardino, California

Susan Kesselring, M.A.
Literacy Educator
Rosemount-Apple Valley-Eagan (Minnesota) School District

PICTURE WINDOW BOOKS
Minneapolis, Minnesota

Max has a great smile.

Max takes good care of his teeth.

He brushes two times every day.

Max goes to the dentist for a checkup.

Dentist

The dentist puts a paper napkin on Max.

The dentist cleans his teeth.

The dentist checks his teeth for cavities.

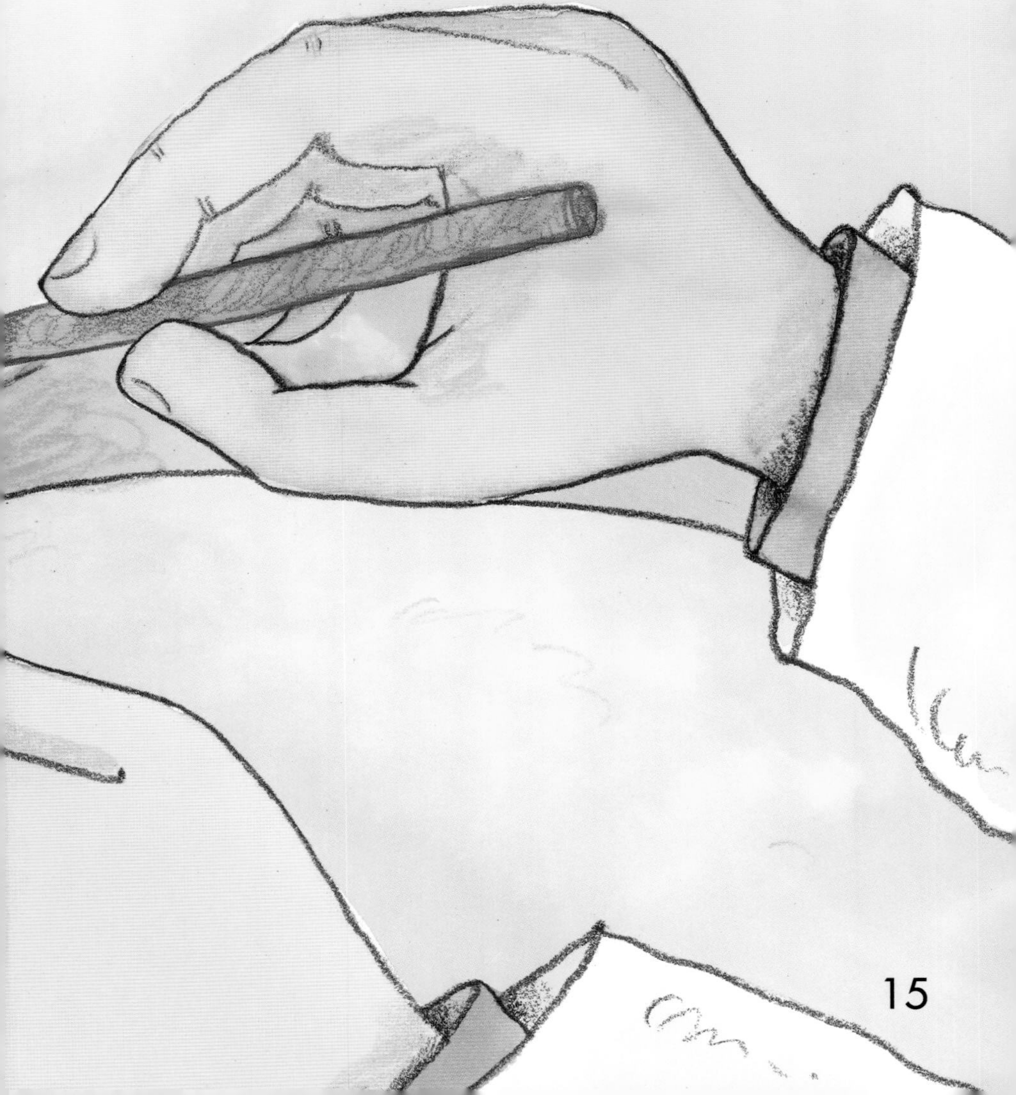

The dentist looks at x-rays of his teeth.

The dentist smiles at Max.

Max had a good checkup.

The dentist gives Max a new toothbrush.

Max looks in the mirror.

Max has a great smile.

WAIT!

DON'T CLOSE THE BOOK!

THERE'S MORE!

FIND MORE:

Games & Puzzles
Heroes & Villains
Authors & Illustrators

AT...

www.CAPSTONEKIDS.com

STILL WANT MORE?

Find cool websites and more books like this one at www.FACTHOUND.com.
Just type in the BOOK ID: 9781404811812 and you're ready to go!